The Day I Was Rich

BILL COSBY

LITTLE BILL BOOKS FOR BEGINNING READERS

The Day I Was Rich

by Bill Cosby

Illustrated by Varnette P. Honeywood

SCHOLASTIC INC. Cartwheel BOOKS ®
New York Toronto London Auckland Sydney

Assistants to art production: Rick Schwab, Nick Naclerio

Library of Congress Cataloging-in-Publication Data

Cosby, Bill, 1937-
    The day I was rich / Bill Cosby; illustrated by Varnette P. Honeywood.
      p.   cm.— (Little Bill books for beginning readers)
    "Cartwheel books."
    Summary: While playing stick-can hockey with his friends, Little Bill discovers what he thinks is a diamond and they all start imagining what it will be like to be rich.
        ISBN 0-590-52172-1 (hardcover) 0-590-52173-X (pbk.)
    [1. Wealth—Fiction. 2. Afro-Americans—Fiction.] I. Honeywood, Varnette P., ill.
II. Title. III. Series. IV. Series: Cosby, Bill, 1937- Little Bill books for beginning readers.
PZ7.C8185Day   1999
[Fic] — dc21   98-54266
                                                   CIP
                                                   AC
10 9 8 7 6 5 4 3 2 1   9/9 0/0 01 02 03 04

Printed in the U.S.A   23
First printing, July 1999

To Ennis,
"Hello, friend,"
B.C.

To the Cosby Family,
Ennis's perseverance against the odds
is an inspiration to us all,
V.P.H.

Dear Parent:

Most of us can recall childhood daydreams of finding buried treasure. Kids are always on the alert to discover some "treasure" (buried or not) that will make them rich, at least in their own eyes. Scavenger Hunt is a favorite game, and with their youthful curiosity, children playing outdoors are more likely than adults to be lucky scavengers.

While playing in the park, Little Bill discovers a "diamond" so huge he needs both hands to lift it. Right away, he and his friends have visions of sudden wealth. With growing excitement they talk about what they're going to buy for themselves once they're millionaires. (*Saving* the money isn't mentioned, of course.) The children don't stop to wonder how such a jewel came to be lost, and no one suggests that it might be a good idea to look for its owner. Apparently, they all subscribe to the childish motto "Finders keepers, losers weepers."

It doesn't occur to them that their treasure is much too big to be a real diamond. Maybe their excitement has swept aside their good sense. But when Little Bill's father shows him that the "diamond" is really just a glass paperweight, the children quickly come back to earth. To their credit, they're able to shrug off their disappointment, laugh at themselves, and go back to the park to play.

There's one thing they still don't know. If they *had* found a real diamond, they wouldn't have been allowed to keep it. Little Bill's father would have helped them turn it in to the park's lost-and-found office, or to the police. They wouldn't have gotten rich. But through making the effort to return a lost treasure to its owner, they would have gained the satisfaction of doing the right thing.

Alvin F. Poussaint, M.D.
Clinical Professor of Psychiatry,
Harvard Medical School and
Judge Baker Children's Center,
Boston, MA

Chapter One

I was playing with my friends in the park. My friends are Kiku, Andrew, José, and Michael. Fuschia is both my cousin and my friend.

We found some sticks and cans and played a new game—stick-can hockey. To play the game, you get some sticks and a can. First, everyone had to find a stick that had fallen from a tree.

"You're not allowed to break a branch off a tree. That's against the rules," Fuschia said. Then everybody had to find a can that had been left in the park. Finding six cans took a while. Michael was the last to find one, so we all helped him.

Then we made up the rules of the game. This is how you play. You hit your can to someone else and wait for someone to hit a can to you. Sometimes you have to wait for someone to pass you a can—and sometimes you get six cans at once.

It's a great game. Everyone wins.

I was passing a can to Kiku when my stick broke. The others kept playing while I looked for a new one. I saw the end of a stick. The rest of it was under a pile of trash, so I pulled it. But the stick was stuck. I pulled it harder, and the trash covering it came loose. And there was the biggest diamond in the world! It was so big that I had to pick it up with *both hands*. How much was this worth?

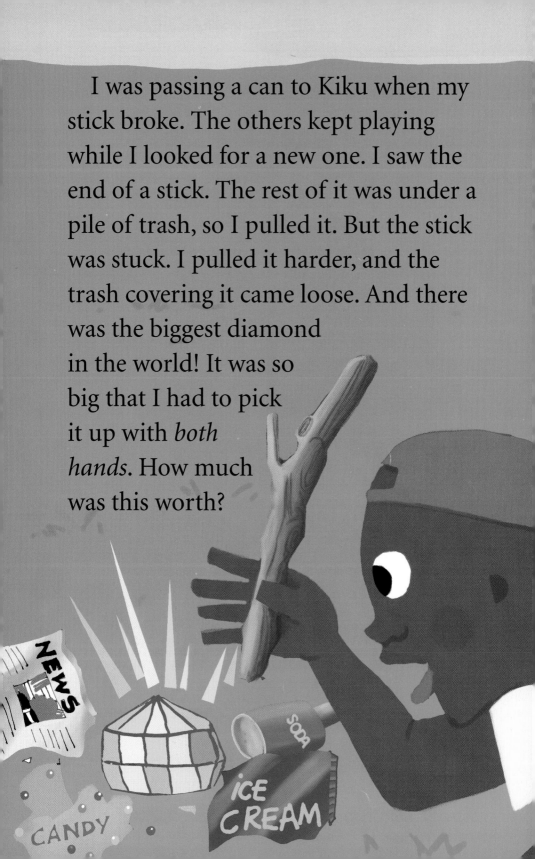

Chapter Two

I yelled to tell the others. "I'm rich! I'm rich!"

My friends stopped playing and ran towards me.

I screamed, "Look what I found! The biggest diamond in the world!"

When my friends saw it, their mouths fell open.

"My mom's diamond is teeny tiny compared to that one," Andrew said. "How much do you think you'll get for it?"

"I don't know," I said. "Maybe five million dollars."

"No way, man!" said Fuschia. "I saw a picture in the paper of a lady wearing a diamond that cost ten million dollars around her neck. This is a skillion times bigger!"

My heart beat fast. More than ten million dollars! I was the richest boy in the world!

"You'd better put that somewhere safe," Fuschia said.

"Yes," I said. "I've got to go home."

We left our cans and sticks and ran to my house as fast as we could.

"You should hide it," Fuschia said.

I held the diamond under my shirt. I kept trying to think cool, but my brain wouldn't stop speeding. I couldn't believe I was so lucky! But I had found it, and it was in my hands and under my shirt!

Chapter Three

We were all breathing hard just thinking about the money.

"What are you going to do with the money?" said Andrew.

"I'm going to give a million dollars to each of you," I said. "Then I'll still have a lot left."

"That diamond is worth about a billion dollars, Little Bill. Could you give us two million?" Andrew said. "If you give me a million dollars, I'll have to pay taxes on it. I've seen my mother and father fill out tax forms—and then they get upset because there isn't enough money to pay the taxes with. If you give us two million, we can use one million to pay our taxes and still have one million left. If you give us only one million, we won't have anything left at all."

"Well, I'll take my million dollars and marry Ms. Correa, my tutor," said José.

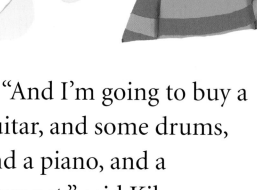

"And I'm going to buy a guitar, and some drums, and a piano, and a trumpet," said Kiku.

"I'm going to buy new sneakers," said Fuschia. "And then I'm going to put a swimming pool and central heating and air conditioning in my cellar. What are you going to do with your money, Little Bill?"

"I'm going to buy a house for my mother—a big house with an indoor swimming pool, and then some new work clothes for my dad. And I'm going to get somebody to make my bed and clean my room like the hotels do. And I'll have a real amusement park with games. And you guys can play for free. Maybe I'll have to move to California because that's where all the big houses are. And you guys can visit me there."

Chapter Four

My father opened the door.

"What's all this heavy breathing about?" he asked.

Everybody was shouting at the same time. My dad's face looked confused.

"What?" he said.

"I found a diamond," I said. "The biggest diamond in the world." I pulled it out from under my shirt. *"And here it is!"*

His eyes opened wide for a second when he saw it, and then his eyelids narrowed. "Oh, Little Bill," he said. "I don't think this is a diamond. I'm sorry."

"You don't?" I asked.

"No, Little Bill," he said. "It's a glass paperweight."

"It is?" I said. "What's a paperweight?"

"It's something you put on top of your papers so they don't blow away," he said.

"Dad, are you sure?" I asked in a small voice. "Are you sure?" I asked again. My voice was even smaller.

"Come with me," he said.

I followed him. It was the slowest walk in my life. I kept wishing that he was wrong.

On his desk was the magnifying glass he used to look at small printing.

He held the diamond in one hand and the magnifying glass in the other and brought them closer to his face. I watched as his eye, magnified by the glass, grew larger.

He examined the diamond, and with a little sadness, he said, "Look here. See the writing on this corner? It says, 'Made in Taiwan.' Diamonds don't have writing on them."

You know what? In just a few minutes, my friends and I were back in the park with our sticks and cans and having a good old time.

We would stop and laugh at how we were fooled and how quickly we ran to my house. And we laughed at how funny we had acted. We must have had a skizillion laughs!

Bill Cosby is one of America's best-loved storytellers, known for his work as a comedian, actor, and producer. His books for adults include *Fatherhood*, *Time Flies*, *Love and Marriage*, and *Childhood*. Mr. Cosby holds a doctoral degree in education from the University of Massachusetts.

Varnette P. Honeywood, a graduate of Spelman College and the University of Southern California, is a Los Angeles-based fine artist. Her work is included in many collections throughout the United States and Africa and has appeared on adult trade book jackets and in other books in the Little Bill series.

Books in the LITTLE BILL series:

The Best Way to Play
None of the parents will buy the new *Space Explorers* video game. How can Little Bill and his friends have fun without it?

The Day I Was Rich
Little Bill has found a giant diamond and now he's the richest boy in the world. How will he and his friends spend all that money?

The Meanest Thing to Say
All the kids are playing a new game. You have to be mean to win it. Can Little Bill be a winner...and be nice, too?

Money Troubles
Funny things happen when Little Bill tries to earn some money.

My Big Lie
Little Bill's tiny fib grew and grew and GREW into a BIG lie. And now Little Bill is in BIG trouble.

One Dark and Scary Night
Little Bill can't fall asleep! There's something in his closet that might try to get him.

Shipwreck Saturday
All by himself, Little Bill built a boat out of sticks and a piece of wood. The older boys say that his boat won't float. He'll show them!

Super-Fine Valentine
Little Bill's friends are teasing him! They say he's *in love*! Will he get them to stop?

The Treasure Hunt
Little Bill searches his room for his best treasure. What he finds is a great big surprise!

The Worst Day of My Life
On the worst day of his life, Little Bill shows his parents how much he loves them. And he changes a bad day into a good one!